A while ago Anna and I decided to draw a map of Tashi's village, just for fun. We know that the Wicked Baron's house is down by the river and that Wise-as-an-Owl lives on the edge of the village.

'What about Chintu?' said Anna, as she marked in his castle. 'It's a long time since we had a story about Chintu the Giant.'

'Yes, I wonder what he's been up to. You do remember that Chintu has a brother who is an even greater menace that he is?' I asked.

'So he does! Let's make him really greedy and gross.' And that's exactly what we did.

ANNA AND BARBARA FIENBERG

Anna and Barbara Fienberg write the Tashi stories together, making up all kinds of daredevil adventures and tricky characters for him to face. Lucky he's such a clever Tashi.

Kim Gamble is one of Australia's favourite illustrators for children. Together Kim and Anna have made such wonderful books as *The Magnificent Nose and Other Marvels*, *The Hottest Boy Who Ever Lived*, the *Tashi* series, the *Minton* picture books, *Joseph,* and a full colour picture book about their favourite adventurer, *There once was a boy called Tashi.*

First published in 2000
This edition first published in 2006

Allen & Unwin
83 Alexander St
Crows Nest NSW 2065
Australia
Phone: (61 2) 8425 0100
Fax: (61 2) 9906 2218
Email: info@allenandunwin.com
Web: www.allenandunwin.com

National Library of Australia
Cataloguing-in-Publication entry:

Fienberg, Anna.
    Tashi and the big stinker.

    New cover ed.
    For primary school children.
    ISBN 978 1 74114 971 5.

    ISBN 1 74114 971 1.

    1. Children's stories, Australian. 2. Tashi (Fictitious character) – Juvenile
    fiction. I. Fienberg, Barbara. II. Gamble, Kim. III. Title. (Series: Tashi; 7).

A823.3

Cover and series design by Sandra Nobes
Typeset in Sabon by Tou-Can Design
Printed in Australia by McPhersons Printing Group

10 9 8 7 6 5 4 3 2

Tashi

and the
BIG
STINKER

written by
Anna Fienberg
and
Barbara Fienberg
•
illustrated by
Kim Gamble

ALLEN&UNWIN

'What kind of sandwiches have you got today, Tashi?' asked Jack.

'Egg,' said Tashi.

'Oh.' Jack pulled at some weeds growing under the bench. There were only ten minutes until the bell.

5

It was a dull kind of day, thought Jack. The sky was grey all over. There wasn't a single dragon or battleship or wicked face in the clouds. And then Tashi had been busy taking a boy to the sick bay—Angus Figment had been bitten by a strange green spider which made Angus's finger go all black and dead-looking. Tashi said it needed urgent treatment, so they hadn't even had time to play.

'Dragon Egg.'

'What?'

'My sandwich.'

'Ooh, let me see.'

Tashi licked the last crumb from the corner of his mouth. 'Sorry, I just finished—boy, was I hungry! I could have eaten ten thousand and six of them!'

'What do dragon eggs taste like?'

'Salty, and a bit hot, like chilli—your tongue tingles as if it's on fire.'

'Gosh,' said Jack. 'I just had cheese.' He stood up gloomily.

'Once somebody really did swallow ten thousand and six of those eggs. It was terrible. Everyone said that's why there are so few dragons around any more. We were lucky—Third Aunt had already salted away piles of them, just in case.'

Jack sat down. 'In one gulp? Swallowed them, I mean.'

'Oh, sure,' said Tashi, stretching out his legs.

'Who was he? Come on, tell me, we've still got nine minutes before the bell.'

'Well,' said Tashi, throwing his lunch
scraps into the bin, 'it was like this. On a
grey, still afternoon, remarkably like this
one in fact, I was sitting with my friends in
the schoolhouse when suddenly the Magic
Warning Bell began to ring. We all ran
straight home, I can tell you! Our mothers
came in from the fields and our fathers
gathered up the animals and bolted the
doors of their shops. What danger could
there be? I wondered. Was it the war lord,
stung by wasps and gone mad? Was it
blood-thirsty pirates? Ravenous witches?

'The ground began to tremble and the dishes clattered on the shelves. Peeping through a crack in the shutters, I saw a giant striding down the street.'

'Chintu!' yelled Jack. 'Remember how you were prisoner in his house once and Mrs Chintu—'

'It wasn't Chintu, Jack. This giant was almost as wide as he was tall. He swelled out in the middle as if he had a hill under his jumper. Well, he passed our house, thank goodness, but he stopped next door and do you know what? He just lifted the roof off, as easily as you please. He scooped up a whole pig that was roasting on a spit and gobbled it down as he went on his way to the end of the village.

'As soon as the earth stopped shuddering under our feet, everyone ran into the street. They were shouting with fright, telling of their wild escapes from death. "He missed me by a hair," Wu was gasping. "That great foot of his came down like a brick wall, and squashed my poor hens flat."

'"Just as well you were roasting a pig at the time, Mrs Wang," said Wise-as-an-Owl, "otherwise he might have taken you instead." A fearful groan ran through the crowd.

'"My word, yes," said Mrs Wang. "I just heard this morning that two people have disappeared from the village over the river."

'People were still muttering and moaning when the village gossip ran up. Wah! That one practically knows what you're going to say and who you're going to visit before you do!'

'Oh, we used to have a neighbour like that—Mr Bigmouth. He was like the local newspaper.'

'Well, anyway, Mrs Fo—the gossip—shouted over everyone. "My second son's wife's cousin works for Chintu the Giant, and he has just told me that Chintu's Only Brother has come to live with him. My cousin says Only Brother is a hundred times worse than Chintu. He says Only Brother eats from morning to night!" Another moan rippled through the crowd and Wise-as-an-Owl turned to me, just as I knew he would.

'"Tashi," he said, "you are the only one of us who has been to Chintu's castle and managed to leave alive. Do you think that you could go again and find out if this is true?"'

'Oh no,' said Jack. 'You didn't have to go, did you?'

'Well,' said Tashi, 'it was like this. I didn't want to, but then I thought it could be my roof that was lifted next time, and no pig in the courtyard! "All right," I said, "I'll get ready straight away."

'My mother packed some food and a warm scarf in a basket. "Be careful, Tashi," she said, "and give these plums to Mrs Chintu with my best wishes."

'I gave her a hug, and set off. It was a night and a day's hard walking ahead of me but I remembered the way well. When I arrived at Chintu's castle I stopped and listened. There was a great muttering and clanging of spoons and forks coming from the kitchen. I made my way towards it and pushed open the door. (That took a while— giants' doors are heavy!)

'There, in the kitchen, was Mrs Chintu. She was rolling some dough, her face creased with bad temper. I ran over and tugged at her skirt.

'"Well, hello, Tashi," she said, most surprised. "What are you doing here?"

'I told her about Only Brother's visit to the village and how frightened the people all were that he would come again. But when I asked if there was anything she could do to help us, Mrs Chintu threw down her chopper and cried, "I wish there was, Tashi. Only Brother is driving *me* crazy as well. He eats all day long, I never stop cooking, so fussy he is with his food. And he keeps Chintu up drinking till dawn, the both of them singing at the tops of their voices. But whenever I ask Chintu to tell him to go, he says, 'He is my Only Brother, I could never ask him to leave.'"

'Just then Chintu stamped into the kitchen roaring, "Fee fi fo—"

'"Now don't start that all over again," Mrs Chintu snapped. "Here's Tashi come to see us. You remember him, don't you? He's the boy who—"

'"Didn't we eat him?"

'"No," said Mrs Chintu hastily, "that was another boy altogether. Is something the matter?"

'Chintu flopped down like a mountain crumbling. "You know how I've been waiting for the pomegranates to ripen on my tree down by the pond? Well, I just went there to pick some and I found that Only Brother has stripped the tree bare and eaten the lot."

'"I told you he should go," said Mrs Chintu.

'"Now don't *you* start that all over again," Chintu roared and he stamped out.

'"You see," sighed Mrs Chintu, "Only Brother will be here forever."

'"Unless we come up with a cunning scheme," I said. "Now let me think..."

'Mrs Chintu sat me on the table. "You'll think better if you're comfortable," she said.

'I closed my eyes and swung my legs and then an idea came. "Did you say Only Brother was a fussy eater?"

'"Yes, I did. Everything has to be just so, even if he does guzzle it all down in a trice."

'"Well then," I said, "for Step One, when you give him his dinner tonight, make sure that his helpings have four times as much pepper as he likes."

'At dinner time, Only Brother gulped down three or four spoonfuls of stew before he realised how hot and spicy it was. "UGH!" he bellowed. "This stew would burn the tonsils off a warthog! No giant could eat it!"

'Chintu, who had no extra pepper in his dinner, took a spoonful. "What's wrong with it?" he growled. "You probably aren't hungry because you are full of *my* pomegranates."

'The two brothers went to bed, scowling. There was no drinking or singing that night. Good, I thought, now for tomorrow—and Step Two.

'The next morning was Chintu's birthday. Mrs Chintu spent all morning making a magnificent birthday cake. When he saw it, Chintu licked the icing on the top and said, "Now, wife, we must be sure Only Brother doesn't see this before dinnertime! I'll hide it in the cellar."

'I waited until Chintu was out of sight and then went to find Only Brother. I described the beauty of the cake and Only Brother's eyes glistened. "Would you like to see it?" I asked. "Just to look at, not to touch, of course." Only Brother would.

'We went downstairs to the cellar and Only Brother stood before the cake, mouth watering. I quietly slipped away.

'That night, after dinner and presents, Chintu went away to fetch his cake. There was a tremendous, ear-splitting roar. He came upstairs with an empty plate and a frightening scowl.

'"Oh, that," said Only Brother, shrugging his shoulders like boulders. "I meant to have just one little slice, but before I knew it, I had finished every sweet-as-heaven crumb. Mmm, delicious, delectable . . . ah!"

'"I've been looking forward to that cake all day!" Chintu kicked Only Brother out of the way and stomped upstairs to bed. "Only *Bother* should be his name," he hissed under his breath. Another early night.

'Good, I thought, now for tomorrow and Step Three.

'The next morning Chintu went down to the river early and stopped a fishing boat laden with lobsters, octopus and fish. He bought the whole catch and went home to tell his wife. "We will have a wonderful meal tonight—shark fin soup and seafood stew. I have left it all in a net in the river to stay cool—just tell me when you want it."

'But when Mrs Chintu sent him down to get the fish, he found Only Brother had eaten the lot—and one or two fishermen as well. Chintu shook his fist and growled.

'"Oh that," said Only Brother, shrugging his shoulders like boulders. "When Tashi told me about the fish I meant to have just one or two, but before I knew it, I had finished them all. Delicious, delectable...ah!"

'Chintu ground his teeth (it sounded like rocks crashing against each other!) and told his wife she would have to find something else for dinner. But Mrs Chintu and I were already making our preparations. I told her to tip two big sacks of beans into the cooking pot. "We'll have bean stew," I said, "and into Only Brother's bowl we'll put a few handfuls of these special berries and spices that Wise-as-an-Owl gave me."

'Only Brother liked the stew so much he had six big bowls of it. And sure enough, after a while, when he and Chintu were sitting drinking their tea, the beans did their work. "BLATT, BANG, PARF!"

'Great gusts of wind exploded from Only Brother's bottom. They were like bombs going off. And the spices we'd added to his stew made the explosions terribly, horribly smelly.

28

'Chintu threw open the windows and door, beetles curled over on their backs, their legs waving weakly in the air, and the canary dropped off its perch.

'Mrs Chintu ran outside, her apron over her nose. Even I was growing dizzy from trying to hold my breath, and I followed her outside.

'The smell came after us. I wiped my eyes. "How can it be so strong, Mrs Chintu?"

'"Well, Tashi, Only Brother is a giant after all, with a giant-sized bottom that makes a giant-sized smell!"

'Inside the castle Chintu was bellowing, "What a stink! What a pong! This is too much—off you go!" and he pushed his brother out the door. He galloped upstairs and gathered Only Brother's clothes and bag and threw them out the window. "Go and find someone else to keep that great stomach of yours full, why don't you!"

"'I'm glad to go," sneered Only Brother. "The food here doesn't suit me at all. Your wife uses too much pepper and her stew gives me wind. Besides," he added as he picked up his slippers, "there's a dreadful smell in your castle. You should do something about it." And he burped like a volcano erupting.

'Mrs Chintu and I did a little victory dance and then she said, "I think you had better slip away home now, Tashi. I saw Chintu giving you hard looks when Only Brother mentioned that you told him where to find the fish."

'I was only too happy to obey. But when I reached the village and tried to tell the news of Only Brother's going, no one would come out into the street.

'"We can't talk now, Tashi, there is this revolting stink. Can't you smell it? Look, even the trees are wilting!"

'"Oh, that," I said, grinning. "That's Only Brother—and it's the very reason for his leaving!"'

The bell rang out over the playground, and Jack stopped laughing. 'There's our warning to get to class,' he said. 'So, quickly, did the villagers give you a reward?'

Tashi grinned. 'No—do you know what happened? Instead of saying how brave I was to get rid of the fearsome giant, people still moan about the time I caused the terrible smell!'

Just then Angus Figment ran past. He waved, and Tashi saw that his black, dead-looking finger looked healthy again. 'It was texta,' Angus cried. 'Mrs Fitzpatrick washed it.'

Tashi laughed, and Jack blew loud exploding raspberries on his arm all the way back to class.

THE MAGIC FLUTE

'Dad,' said Jack, 'can I ask you something?'

'Sure,' said Dad. 'What's it about—turbo engines, shooting stars, hermit crabs—I'm good at all those subjects!'

'No,' Jack said, 'it's like this. Say your friend is in trouble, but when you go to save him, you hurt the person who got him into trouble. Does that mean you did the wrong thing?'

'Which friend is that, Jack?' said Dad. 'Would it be my mate Charlie over the road, or is it Henry, the one I play cards with?'

'Oh, Dad, it doesn't matter,' sighed Jack. 'It's the idea, see—a question of right or wrong. Or say you owe someone a hundred dollars and...'

'Who owes a hundred dollars?' Mum
came in with three bowls and spoons.

Jack rolled his eyes. 'It doesn't matter
who, Mum! Maybe I'd better tell you the
whole story—just the way Tashi told me.'

'Oh boy, icecream, peaches and a Tashi
story for dessert!' Dad cried gleefully.

'Yes,' said Jack sternly. 'But listen
carefully, because I'll ask you some
questions at the end.'

Dad leant forward, frowning thought-
fully, to show how serious he could be.

'Well,' began Jack, 'back in the old
country, it had been a good summer and
the rice had grown well. People were
looking forward to a big harvest, when a
traveller arrived with dreadful news. The
locusts were coming! In the next valley he'd
seen a great swarm of grasshoppers settle
on the fields in the morning, leaving not
one blade of grass at the end of the day.'

Dad shook his head. 'Awful damage they do, locusts. You can ask me anything about them, son. Anything. They're one of my best subjects.'

'Later,' Jack said. 'Well, the Baron called a meeting in the village square.'

'That sneaky snake!' exploded Dad. 'He diddles everyone out of their money, doesn't he!'

'That's the one,' agreed Jack. 'But now the Baron was very worried because he owned most of the fields, although everyone in the town worked a little vegetable patch or had a share in the village rice fields.

'At the meeting, Tashi's grandfather suggested hosing the crops with poison but there wasn't time to buy it. Someone else said they should cover the fields with sheets, but of course there weren't enough sheets in the whole province to do that. Tashi racked his brains for an idea but nothing came.

'Just when everyone was in despair,
a stranger stepped into the middle of the
square. He was a very odd-looking fellow,
dressed in a rainbow coloured shirt and silk
trousers. On his head was a red cap with a
bell. The people had to blink as they stared
at him—he glowed like a flame.

'"I can save your fields from the
locusts," he said. Tashi looked up
into his eyes. They were pale
and hooded.

'"Can you really? How?" the people shouted as they crowded around. They wanted to believe him, and there was

something about him, this man. You could feel a kind of power that made you think he would deliver whatever he promised to do. But his eyes were full of shadows.

'"What will you need?" asked the Baron.

'"Nothing except my payment," replied the stranger. "You must give me a bag of gold when the locusts have gone."

'The people quickly agreed, and it was just as well they did. Only a moment later the sky began to grow dark and a deep thrumming like a million fingers drumming could be heard.

'Clouds of locusts appeared overhead, clouds so big and black that the sun was blocked completely, and then wah! just like that, the noise stopped and they settled on the village rice fields and gardens.

'But before the locusts could eat a blade
of grass, the stranger brought out his flute
and played a single piercing note. It echoed
in the silence and the locusts quivered.
Six shrill notes followed, and as the last
note sounded, the locusts rose as one, and
flew away to the south. In three minutes the
air was clear.

'There was a stunned silence. People looked at each other, hardly able to believe what they had just seen. Tashi's grandfather ran up to the stranger and shook his hand, thanking him, but the Baron stepped in and cut him off. He gathered the Elders around him, saying, "Let's not be too hasty in our thanks. We can't be sure it was the stranger's flute that drove off the locusts. Maybe they would have gone of their own accord. And, in any case, a bag of gold is far too much to pay for one moment's work."

'When Tashi's father and the Elders disagreed, the Baron went on, "I know none of you has more than a few silver pieces between you, so who do you suppose would have to pay the most of it? Me, of course. Well, I won't do it, and you must all stand by me."

'Tashi felt a shiver of dread. This was the wrong thing to do. He could see that many of the others were unhappy too, and some of them started to argue with the Baron but he brushed them aside. He walked over to the stranger and tossed him a single gold coin, saying, "Here you are, fellow, you earned that coin easily enough."

'The stranger let the coin fall to the ground and slowly looked around at the people. "Do you all agree with him?"

'The people shuffled and looked away.

'"You will be sorry—oh, how very sorry," the stranger said quietly, and he drifted away, the bright flame of him shimmering in the distance.

'On the way home Tashi's grandfather
took his hand and sighed.

'"We did a bad thing today, Tashi. We
robbed that man of his reward."

'"Yes," said Tashi, "and I have a
horrible cold feeling in my tummy telling
me this is not the end of it. There was
something about the way the stranger
looked at us when he left. He's not an
ordinary man, that's for sure."

'Tashi's family said that there was
nothing they could do tonight but that in

the morning they would speak with the Elders. They would find the stranger and promise to pay him, a little at a time.

'Tashi was too restless and worried to sleep. Finally he jumped out of bed and went off to see if Wise-as-an-Owl had returned yet. He had been visiting his Younger Sister who lived in the next village. Surely he would have some good advice.

'And that is why Tashi, alone of all the children in the village, never heard those first beautiful, magical notes from the stranger's flute. The children sat up in bed and listened. They ached to hear more. And soon it seemed that their veins ran with golden music, not blood, and they had to follow those notes to stay alive. Quietly they slipped from their houses and followed the music, out of the town, across the fields and into the forest.

'Next morning there were screams and cries as parents discovered that their children were missing.

'"I knew it! I knew it!" Tashi cried as he ran back into the village. Just then he spied some pumpkin seeds on the road. Hai Ping! Tashi's friend Hai Ping nibbled them all the time, and what's more he'd had a hole in his pocket lately so that he left a trail of seeds wherever he went. Without a word Tashi set off, out of the town, across the fields and into the forest.

'As the darkness of the trees closed around him, Tashi heard the faint notes of the sweetest, most lovely melody. It was like Second Cousin's finest dark chocolate dissolved into air. It made his mouth water, his ears ache, his heart pump quickly. And his fears of the stranger came flooding back. Now he knew why he'd been so uneasy about the piper. There was a story his grandmother once told him about a piper and a plague of rats. Tashi bent down and scooped up some clay to stuff into his ears. It was the hardest thing he'd ever done. He closed his eyes as the sounds of the music and forest died away.

'The pumpkin seeds had been getting harder to find and now they stopped altogether. But Tashi continued along the path, following clues he'd learned to read— a broken twig, a thread caught on a thorn bush. At last, through the trees, he saw two little boys. They were the smallest of the village children and were straggling behind. They mouthed something which Tashi couldn't hear, and pointed up ahead.

'Tashi saw the other children nearing the top of the hill. Suddenly he realised where they were all heading and his blood froze. The path ended in a sheer drop, down, down, a hundred metres down to the rushing waters of a mountain gorge. The piper was playing the flute while the children streamed past him—towards the cliff. He was playing them to their deaths! Wah!

'Tashi raced up and burst out of the bushes. He butted the piper over, knocking the flute out of his hands. The children stopped, their eyes no longer blank, their minds no longer bewitched. Slowly they gathered around as Tashi and the stranger struggled towards the edge of the drop.

'"The piper was leading you over this cliff!" Tashi gasped. The children formed a wall and closed in on the piper.

'With a desperate pull, Tashi broke free
from the stranger and rolled away towards
the flute, which was lying half-hidden in the
grass. He picked it up and hurled it with all
his strength out over the cliff edge.

'The stranger gave a groan of rage but Tashi cried, "It wasn't the children's fault that you weren't paid. You had better go quickly before our parents come."

'The stranger looked up at the stony faces of the children and he shrugged. They moved aside to let him pass and all watched silently as he disappeared into the forest.

'The children met the search party of parents on the way back to the village and they told them what had happened. Some parents wept, and they looked at each other with shame.

'"Just think," they said, "but for Tashi, we would have been too late."

'The Baron kept very busy away from the village for the next few weeks and when he did finally return, he looked rather guilty and was so polite that people thought he must be sickening for something. But he was soon back to tricking people out of their wages and charging too much for his watermelons again, so life went on as before.'

'Blasted Baron!' cried Dad. 'He's got the morals of a dung beetle!'

'Worse. Dung beetles do some very good work,' put in Mum.

'But don't you see,' said Jack. 'It wasn't right that the piper never got paid—'

'But he was about to do a very dreadful thing!'

'But if he hadn't been treated badly in the first place—'

'Well,' said Mum, clearing away the dishes, 'people have been discussing what's right and wrong for centuries—and we've only got half an hour before *The Magic Pudding*'s on.'

'Yeah,' agreed Dad. 'Why don't you ask me about turbo engines—they don't take so long, and they take you far!'

Jack grinned. 'The day Tashi found a pair of magic shoes, he travelled 100 kilometres in one leap!'

'No, really?' cried Dad. Then his face dropped. 'But I bet that's another story, right?'

'Right,' laughed Jack. 'And now, Dad, the clock's ticking. What would you have done if *you* were the piper?'